I0640956

Firebrand Firestorm

The Ancestors of Bjorn Esterday

Volume 13

Deliverance

July 4, 1776

Wynter Sommers

This work is registered with the UK Copyright Service, in accordance with the Copyright, Designs and Patents Act 1988
All rights reserved 284718040

USA Copyright © 2015 GJ dePillis
© 2015, TXu001966602 / 2015-05-08 and TXu001983965 / 2015-11-04

Library of Congress Control Number: 2020943167

Published by Pure Force Enterprises, Inc.
California, USA
Since 2002

INGRAM

INGRAM® Distribution

ISBN-13: 978-1-7184-0025-2
ISBN-10: 1-7184-0025-X

DEDICATION

To those who feel strongly about truth,
justice, and the integrity of America:
your honorable actions make us proud.
To those who wonder if their daily
choices matter: your small decisions
impact generations to come.
To those everyday people who don't think
they have what it takes: when you strive
for extraordinary things, the impossible
becomes reality.
Your dreams today become our future
tomorrow.
Thank you for everything you do.

Bjorn Esterday
Was Not Born Yesterday
Series

Firebrand (15 Volumes+Conversation Station Book)
Edges (9 Stories +Conversation Station Book)
Gone (18 Stories + Conversation Station Book)

Bjorn EDGES Series

EDGES Book 1-Swift Encounter
EDGES Book 2-Rousing Attack
EDGES Book 3-One Foot Under
EDGES Book 4-Earthshake
EDGES Book 5-Broken String
EDGES Book 6-Key Witness
EDGES Book 7-Who is She?
EDGES Book 8-Vanish
EDGES Book 9-Chase or Die

Bjorn Series Alternate Reading Plan

1st	Edges Book 1		22nd	Gone Book 10
2nd	Edges Book 2		23rd	Firebrand Vol 9
3rd	Gone Book 1		24rd	Gone Book 11
4th	Firebrand Vol 1		25th	Firebrand Vol 10
5th	Edges Book 3		26th	Gone Book 12
6th	Firebrand Vol 2		27th	Gone Book 13
7th	Gone Book 2		28th	Firebrand Vol 11
8th	Gone Book 3		29th	Gone Book 14
9th	Firebrand Vol 3		30th	Firebrand Vol 12
10th	Gone Book 4		31st	Gone Book 15
11th	Firebrand Vol 4		32nd	Firebrand Vol 13
12th	Gone Book 5		33rd	Gone Book 16
13th	Gone Book 6		34th	Firebrand Vol 14
14th	Edges Book 4		35th	Gone Book 17
15th	Firebrand Vol 5		36th	Firebrand Vol15 (End)
16th	Gone Book 7		37th	Gone Book 18 (End)
17th	Firebrand Vol 6		38th	Edges Book 5
18th	Gone Book 8		39th	Edges Book 6
19th	Firebrand Vol 7		40th	Edges Book 7
20th	Gone Book 9		41st	Edges Book 8
21st	Firebrand Vol 8		42nd	Edges Book 9(End)

ACKNOWLEDGMENTS

We acknowledge those who actively build peace. We acknowledge all the selfless talent which contributed to creating meaningful tokens of consideration and sharing. We acknowledge that every person has a daily choice of right or wrong... and we thank you for choosing the right, good, honorable path filled with integrity because that is the difficult and brave path. Small choices today become lasting monuments of loving hope tomorrow.

CONTENTS

0 PREFACE

So many things. Rain. Boats. Fire... and now it is July 3rd, 1776. What will happen next?

Is Bryce Aiden Tyler motivated by integrity? Is that why he is trying to help those in distress? What will happen to everyone on the ship? What will Bryce be willing to sacrifice for helping people he does not know? Would you make such a sacrifice? Have you ever felt so focused on an heroic act that you ignored a looming danger?

In a culture where swimming lessons are unheard of, would you rush in to save people from a sinking boat, knowing if you fell overboard you would undoubtedly come to a grievous end? Would you follow your friend into danger as Eliza did with Jane? How would you feel if you tried, but could not save your friend? Would you be satisfied to know that your efforts actually did save other lives... even if it was not that of your friend? Would praise from a stranger console you in your grief?

If you were Polly, stranded, helpless, in a strange Inn during a fierce storm, what would you think if you were having a baby without your husband being near-by? Would you focus on loving your newborn babe? Or would you focus on the circumstances over which you have no control?

1 CHAPTER 129: (JULY 4, 1776) Room For One More

"But Polly is with child!" Susanna protested as she addressed Silversmith.

Susanna had already climbed into Billy Dawes' carriage and Silversmith had just alerted Polly about needing her German translation and English copy of the document. Billy Dawes was checking the bridles on his horses as he knew he was about to embark on a furiously speedy journey across storm wrecked roads.

Silversmith, pleased she could be truly helpful to Susanna Wright, and that Susanna had even complimented her on her plan, was concentrating on each detail to ensure it operated smoothly. Silversmith noticed this about herself. If praised, she tended to work even more fervently on the task before her, blocking out all else.

The furious storm had finally passed and the rain had stopped. After checking the horses, and combing his hair with his fingers and one of the horse brushes, Billy Dawes ascended the carriage and sat at his post as he situated his cap. He was waking himself up along with his mighty steeds as he grabbed for the reins, awaiting the passengers to load themselves.

Polly, layered in fabric, emerged from the door of the Inn. Silversmith tried to explain to Susanna Wright as Polly approached.

Silversmith shared, "Miss Wright, Polly had her child last night and she told me she wrote it and she insists on delivering it herself."

Susanna shook her head, "You mean she won't rest as she should and she won't trust us to deliver the documents to be signed?" Susanna summarized.

"Indeed, Miss Wright," Silversmith affirmed, "Miss Polly won't let that document leave her sight."

"But," Susanna firmly protested, "who will take proper care of the newborn babe? The rough roads after a storm is no place for Polly, nor her delicate newborn."

Billy Dawes silently observed all the interactions from his perch, yet remained silent.

Silversmith explained, "She's bringing the babe with her. I can mind it in the carriage whilst you interact with the menfolk." Silversmith offered as she evaluated the available space inside the carriage.

"I think there is enough room. It will fit a new mother and her babe, as well as the two of us."

Billy called from his perch, "The carriage is large enough to accommodate..." and then he stopped.

Billy realized he probably should have remained silent as Susanna Wright leaned out of the carriage and looked up at him with a stern gaze. Billy quickly added, "the power of six horses..."

Reluctant, Susanna Wright acquiesced, "Very well. We have turned into a rather large travelling committee, I fear. Right now it does appear to be an unusually mild mid-summery day. Sixty Eight to seventy degrees, I think the thermometer read. Contrary to the Dog Days star rising. It is not as hot and humid as I would expect, so it is a welcoming day for a newborn babe."

Surprising Susanna from the other side of the Carriage, Mrs. Dunlap thumped on the window.

"Hello," Mrs. Dunlap sang cheerfully.

Susanna, startled, turned suddenly toward the loud noise. "Hello?" she repeated.

Mrs. Dunlap walked around to the door of the carriage and explained to Susanna, "Oh, I'm Mrs. Dunlap. My husband is the printer who type set the document Polly translated." She indiscreetly noted, "He is awaiting my word to print and distribute as soon as we have this copy signed," Mrs. Dunlap sighed as she comically attempted to board the carriage, "So, you see it is imperative I come along, as well."

Billy Dawes was about to dismount to assist these new passengers, but Mrs. Dunlap, waved him away, shouting, "You must stay at the reins, Mr. Dawes, as our departure is rapidly forthcoming."

As Mrs. Dunlap climbed into the carriage, with the aid of Silversmith, Mrs. Dunlap said, "Besides, should Polly become faint, I should be there."

Mrs. Dunlap made herself comfortable as she in a tone which implied refusal of her self-invitation would be tantamount to an etiquette faux pas.

"I suppose the carriage is large enough for one more..." Susanna acquiesced as Silversmith also assisted Polly to enter the carriage, along with her newborn babe.

"Oh, I can't wait to see Jane's face! She will be so proud of us!" Mrs. Dunlap enthused.

"Perhaps we should also be there," Eunice suggested, appearing from nowhere, yet fully dressed in a simple doe-skin dress. "My son and I were instrumental with introducing a new life into this world."

Mrs. Dunlap responded to Susanna Wright's confused expression and fostered an introduction as Eunice boarded the carriage.

Mrs. Dunlap looked at Silversmith and

at Susanna Wright and explained,

"This lady is Eunice Marguerite Kanenstenhawi Arosen."

She spoke as she accepted the newborn babe into her arms while Polly situated herself as best she could in the carriage.

Mrs. Dunlap continued, "She may be Mrs. Arosen... but insists on being called Eunice... a charming name, indeed."

"Eunice, please... I prefer an informal greeting as if we are long-time friends." Eunice nodded to support Mrs. Dunlap's introduction.

"Oh!" Mrs. Dunlap added to explain, "The storm last night delayed travel for many... Including Eunice and her son, TallMan here... If I couldn't find a midwife, I was going to retrieve a medicine man. Polly required immediate attention, as you can see," Mrs. Dunlap indicated the healthy babe bundled and sleeping soundly.

"TallMan?" Susanna Wright uttered with a bewildered tone, "Medicine man? Another person?" Susanna asked as the passengers, now cramped, tried to pat down their skirts so as to not fill the entire carriage compartment.

"I can ride up with Mr. Dawes," Silversmith offered as Billy Dawes smiled at the idea and extended a helpful arm to hoist Silversmith up to sit next to him.

"A pleasure to meet you, Miss Wright," TallMan said as he looked inside the carriage. "Since this is the baby's first exposure to the public, I should be nearby to address any mishaps, should they arise." He said as he tapped a bag, presumably filled with medicine.

Noticing the crowded skirts, and wanting to provide Polly privacy should her baby awaken and need feeding, TallMan called up to Billy Dawes, who was now sitting next to Silversmith atop the carriage.

TallMan asked, "Is there room for one more?"

Billy replied, "Join us and then we shall depart." Billy Dawes invited the very tall medicine man with a friendly wave of his hand. .

In one step, TallMan reached the top and sat on the other side of Billy Dawes, sandwiching Mr. Dawes between Silversmith and the bulk of TallMan himself.

Now, with elbows squished to his sides, Billy Dawes inhaled slowly, trying not to push off either TallMan nor Silversmith. He leaned forward and with a flick of his wrists, snapped the reins on the six steeds pulling the carriage. With a chorus of soprano squeals escaping from the cabin of the carriage, Billy galloped away.

Eunice, Mrs. Dunlap, Susanna Wright, Polly and the newborn babe, all safely inside the carriage and Silversmith, TallMan and Billy Dawes on the driver's bench, atop the carriage, were all about to embark on an exciting new, albeit loosely formed, journey... and Susanna still had not informed the occupants that their friends Jane and Bryce Aiden Tyler were lost at sea.

Susanna evaluated the situation and decided to wait to share the sad news until after the document was signed.

2 CHAPTER 130: (JULY 4, 1776) Bryce At Sea

Eliza wrapped herself tighter in her scratchy wool blanket, as she looked out to the horizon beyond the docks. She did not stray from the Magistrate's side. She felt his presence provided great comfort.

Before her, lay the ocean, now calm that the storm had passed, but behind her lay the exhausted crumpled survivors sprawled out across the dock. They were lucky to be alive, thanks to

13

the heroic foolhardy boldness of Mr. Bryce Aiden Tyler.

Both Eliza and the Magistrate gazed out onto the horizon, hoping that somehow he might return. "I worry that Susanna went without me," Eliza Lucas shared with Magistrate Karl Pinkney.

Magistrate Pinkney replied with logic, "My man could not have carried more than one on horseback and you are in no condition for travel, Miss Lucas."

"Seeing him dash off with Susanna reminded me of my father..." Eliza mused, "Oh, how I hope someday we will have the sort of change which will prevent people from profiting from a broken design... All these innocents yanked from their homes to be sold as slaves for greed? My father would try to do something to stop it from happening ever again."

Magistrate Pinkney replied, "Is your father a military man?" He turned fully toward her speaking in soothing tones,

"Perhaps you could tell me stories of him... It would help to pass the time as we both wait... Eliza..." He smiled kindly toward her.

"I am indeed comforted by your presence... Karl..." Eliza Lucas admitted with an impish grin.

"I am comforted by your company, as well... Eliza," Magistrate Karl Pinkney smiled as he walked slowly along the docks with Eliza at his side.

Magistrate Pinkney continued to check the tethering of each row boat his men had borrowed along the harbor. He wanted to anchor or tether them to their original slips so their rightful owners would find them in working order. No damage had been suffered by the tiny bobbing vessels.

Eliza pointed to an empty spot, "That boat is missing. Was it lost at sea during the storm?"

Magistrate Pinkney replied, "No, Miss Lucas. I sent the Wine Merchant's boat back out to try and search for Bryce, my friend."

Eliza replied, "You mean just in case?"

Karl Pinkney replied, "Yes. If there is only a ten percent chance of survival, then I shall take it... as he would have done if our places were reversed..."

Eliza observed, "You are right to hope for the best..."

The Magistrate lamented, "All this could have been avoided if the greed of Henry Mossop and Tweedbottom was stopped earlier."

"You cannot assume all the responsibility of trying to reverse what has already happened in the past," Eliza soothed. "You did not lose any men during the storm. This is something to be thankful for..."

"All my men are accounted for, save Bryce..." he responded.

Magistrate Pinkney looked out to the horizon. He squinted into the rising sun, "I see a boat approaching, perhaps with news..." He inhaled the distinctive scents of salty seaweed and then exhaled slowly, anticipating the arrival of the vessel, "We shall soon ascertain if Bryce was found... dead or alive..."

Slowly...too slowly, the boat approached the dock.

3 CHAPTER 131: (JULY 4, 1776-6:00am) Feather

"Have you selected a name for the babe?" Susanna Wright asked Polly as they bumped along in the carriage.

Billy Dawes, TallMan and Silversmith were on top of the carriage and Susanna, Polly, Mrs. Dunlap, and Eunice were closely positioned inside. Only the skirts of Mrs. Dunlap invaded the laps of the other ladies.

The babe slept peacefully in Polly's arms, as she smiled, "Not yet."

18

"Unusual," Mrs. Dunlap commented, "I've seen many a babe. I would expect it to be upset and crying in a bumpy ride such as this. Yet, he dreams so peacefully."

"Perhaps, he is destined," Eunice observed, "to keep his wits about him during times of anxiety. If he does not grow to become a man of leadership, one of his descendants shall. He will solve problems."

"Problems!" Polly announced, "Mrs. Dunlap. I have packed the documents, both English and German. I even have a bottle of ink, yet I forgot the quill! I left it in the guest room at the Inn!"

"Oh, my!" Mrs. Dunlap fretted, "How will they sign it?"

"We are all ladies of this New World," Eunice interjected, "and we will solve this problem." She thumped on the roof of the carriage.

The horses slowed from a gallop to a trot. From a trot to a walk. From a walk to a full stop. The horses snorted while they caught their breath and welcomed the respite.

"Eunice," Susanna Wright explained, "With all due respect, time is of the essence, here. We have not the time to stop. We mustn't be late!"

Eunice advised, "One cannot rush into a solution. Inhale and take a moment to solve the problem early before it becomes exacerbated. Then one can resume at full force. Otherwise all your efforts will be for naught," Eunice cautioned.

TallMan opened the door.

"Why have you wished for Billy Dawes to stop the carriage?" TallMan asked.

"I would like to know the same thing..." Susanna muttered as she leaned her head back against the wall, defeated.

Eunice said, "Haliaeetuleucocephalus."

Mrs. Dunlap, Polly and Susanna Wright looked at Eunice perplexed, yet TallMan seemed to understand her perfectly. He reached inside his belt and pulled out a knife.

Susanna and Polly gasped.

Mrs. Dunlap tried to lessen the tension felt by Susanna Wright by sharing, "Oh, he gets that reaction quite a bit."

Then, TallMan pulled a single feather from his belt and used his knife to fashion a sharp nib on the quill of the feather. He then followed his mother Eunice's glance, and handed the implement to Polly with a sharp nod.

"You requested a pen... made of the feather of an eagle," TallMan stated simply.

"The master of flight," Eunice explained, "With the brave head as pure as snow and a wingspan up to seven and a half feet wide. Your new pen is from the king of the skies. Fitting, I think."

"A brave and majestic creature to symbolize our mission," Susanna concurred.

"Better than a turkey feather, which is what I would have used..." Mrs. Dunlap commented.

TallMan mentioned, "Pliny the Elder, the ancient medicine man of Europe, wrote of five animals representing Roman legions of infantry. The wolf, Minotaur, horse, boar and of course the eagle."

TallMan paused to verify they were listening. He drew a breath and continued, "Later, only the eagle embodied the ultimate standard to which all others must aspire. The Roman warrior holding the symbol of the eagle directed others in battle... Much as you want the people of these colonies to follow their Colonial Representatives as they sign your Declaration with this feather given to me by the eagle who used to proudly wear it as it soared in the skies above, surveying his territory."

"His territory?" Polly asked.

Eunice clarified, "or her territory. It could have been dropped from the heavens by a female eagle."

TallMan handing Polly the quill with polite, respectful, yet efficient ceremony.

Polly accepted the feather with appreciation. "Thank you, TallMan for the thoughtful gesture and eloquent story. The Declaration document, which I copied, is not requesting a Rome with a Caesar."

"No?" TallMan softly clarified.

"Quite the opposite, actually," Polly explained with an impish smile. "I do, however, appreciate that this feather stands for meeting the highest standards of quality, and I think it is quite fitting."

Pleased with the positive reactions, TallMan smiled, closed the door behind him, and silently bounded up to the wooden perch to reclaim his seat next to the driver, Billy Dawes who was still seated next to Silversmith. The carriage bounced a bit as it settled under the weight of TallMan's ascent.

A moment later, Billy snapped the reins and the horses started to walk, then trot and with a "heeeeeyah!" Billy urged the horses into a gallop. The ladies inside remained speechless.

Except for Eunice who commented, "Problem resolved."

4 CHAPTER 132: (JULY 4, 1776 3:00AM) FLASHBACK Churning Waters-Hours earlier

The storm had been ferocious, whipping the boats around like a hungry lion shaking its prey before devouring it.

Although the winds had calmed, the seas still churned.

Bryce Aiden Tyler, temporary captain of the wine merchant's boat, kept his eye on the smoldering inferno, which was once The Spy vessel.

Bryce kept his knees loose as he had to get up close to one of the men and shout to be heard.

"Did you tie all the cork sacs together onto the rope?" Bryce yelled as pins of water pelted his face.

"Aye, sir. Survivors just need to grab the rope or a cork sac and we can then pull 'em all aboard and head to the dock for shelter and then return to collect more." The red-coated soldier, appointed to assist Bryce Aiden Tyler by Magistrate Pinkney, shouted in reply.

The wine merchant's boat was no match for the violent haphazard lapping of water pummeling the deck, making it slippery. A new appreciation for sailors and fishermen permeated the thoughts of all those aboard the wine merchant's boat.

The cork-dotted rope, now being lowered into the water, fought against the tides and started to return to the wine merchant's boat, tangling around the rudder instead of moving forward toward the bobbing blazing Colonial slave transport ship.

Horrified that his brilliant idea had gone awry so quickly, and was now further endangering the men who had volunteered to help rescue the others, Bryce Aiden Tyler had to make a decision. Quickly.

If nothing were done, the wine merchant's boat would be food for the sea monsters who lived below the surface. Biting his lip, Bryce shot a glance from bow to stern, evaluating options. This vessel was never built for rugged seas, let alone rescue. What could be done to prevent the deaths of everyone aboard this commandeered vessel?

Bryce's suspicions were confirmed

"Sir!" One crimson-coated volunteer staggered to Bryce Aiden Tyler, "Your rope in the water. See?" He pointed over the dark waters, "It's clumping and knotting up. That twisted rope could cause us to capsize."

"We cannot," Bryce declared, "help others until we steady ourselves...'Twas my idea to save one soul, but not to jeopardize so many others. She may already be dead, so I must be the one to right this chaos." Bryce pulled off his boots and jacket.

"We need a sail. Men, unbutton your jackets," Bryce shouted to the exhausted volunteers aboard the wine merchant's boat, "line up side-by-side. Face the water, all around the railing. On my command, open your jackets and coats wide to catch the wind and push me closer... Unbutton your overcoats and Jackets."

"Sir?" the men questioned.

"On my mark..." Bryce shouted ignoring the doubts in their voices. Bryce barked the order, "Now!"

Some men wore coats over their

uniformed jackets. Others had only their red uniforms. All quickly unbuttoned them.

Once Bryce cried out, they all faced the water in a line, side-by-side in the direction Bryce indicated. Then, they opened their jackets, or shoved their hands into the pockets and stretched their arms wide like bats about to take flight. They turned their faces away from the venomous bites of the ocean winds.

The wine merchant's vessel responded.

It slowly inched closer to where Bryce wanted to go, and away from the clumping mass of rope. Then Bryce Aiden Tyler, temporary wine merchant boat captain, shouted the order to cease. The men relaxed their arms and started to button up again.

Before the men could turn around to ask why Bryce had done what he had just done, Bryce jumped overboard into the dark churning waters.

5 CHAPTER 133: (JULY 4, 1776-3:05am) Bryce Splashed

"Why did Mr. Tyler jump overboard?" The confused red coated volunteers aboard the wine merchant's boat asked each other. Nobody had an answer to explain his rash movement.

"Look!" One volunteer pointed into the waters and shouted, "He's untangling the rope. He's pulling the rope away from our rudder." The others clustered around him to see for themselves.

Another volunteer shouted to the

group, "We now can return back to the docks, but I say we stay here and wait for Mr. Tyler to return. Are we in agreement?"

One replied, "We must hope he returns soon. This vessel shan't withstand many more beatings! What is the purpose of tying all those cork-filled sacs to the rope? Why is he swimming away from us? Should he not be boarding the vessel now that we have been untangled?"

Another replied, "The cork sacs keep the rope afloat. That means if there be survivors in the water, they can grab a bag to remain above surface."

"So," The first responded, "Then the rowboats can fetch them so the victims can board our wine merchant's boat?"

The latter replied, "Yes. Or perhaps the rowboats will bring them back to the docks directly."

Another shouted, "If Mr. Tyler can get to the victims before they drown... How could he manage before he himself sinks from exhaustion?"

On deck, one man grabbed a mop and kept pushing water off the deck as soon as it had splashed on. Three rushed to guard the helm and steady the wheel. Yet another took to ensuring the sails were in the proper direction and another checked below deck to make sure there were no leaks. Others took up tasks to ensure the wine merchant's boat remained afloat until Bryce Aiden Tyler returned.

One man asked another, "The Spy. Wasn't she supposed to warn those of us stationed here in the British Americas?"

"If she was, their officers didn't do a very good job of it," another replied.

"Perhaps that's why the Spy ship was captured. The British navy didn't think she was significant enough to guard."

"But," another commented, "to let a fine vessel like that be stolen and then be used for the dastardly purpose of transporting kidnapped colonists? That is what Mr. Tyler told me on our way out to this spot. Said his business partner was working on stopping it... Halting that vessel from departing from the docks."

Four men worked to lower the anchor so they would remain at this exact location when Bryce returned. Fortunately, they were not far from shore.

The volunteer crew resumed speculations as to the original purpose of the Spy. "Or perhaps it was shipping cargo which would give King George more gold"

"Are you suggesting the Spy's original purpose was to rescue slaves, not collect and sell them?" the other shouted as they felt the anchor hit bottom. "Light a lantern so Mr. Tyler can spot us", he ordered, "not a torch, it may blow out again... a lantern to protect the flame."

6 CHAPTER 134: (JULY 4, 1776 3:10AM to 5:00AM) – Bryce Bobbing In Water

After Bryce dove overboard into the uncharacteristically cold waters on this summer dawn, he forced his limbs to work. During the heat of the summer, this surprising isolated storm startled everybody. It was as if the finger of God had reached down to punish a great injustice.

Finally, Bryce's hand found the bulk of the rope, still floating on the surface thanks to those cork-filled sacs the men had tied to it earlier. He used it to guide himself to the tangled mass, which threatened the Wine Merchant's boat.

He noticed the men had started to drop anchor. Relieved that the boat would wait for his return, Bryce worked on untangling the massive ropes, which floated dangerously near the rudder, preventing it from operating, as it should.

Next, he pulled the length of the rope and swam over toward the still blazing inferno, which was once the Spy ship. As he neared the vessel, he looked up and saw the huge lettering S-P-Y above him.

Around him, floating on the water's surface, were bits of flaming debris, which had fallen from the ship.

Then, he heard a noise and as he looked up to the name of the ship above him, he saw a portion of it was weakening and loosening. Then, it tipped outward and snapped off, falling down on top of Bryce with a huge splash.

By chance, Bryce Aiden Tyler had sufficient warning of the impending crash. He filled his lungs with air as he retreated beneath the surface mere seconds before impact.

The sound of the planks hitting the salt water made a loud noise, which, Bryce could hear, muffled, as he held his breath under the water.

The soft sizzle of the fiery edges being extinguished by the water signaled to Bryce that he could resurface and refill his lungs with much needed air.

From under the surface of the water, Bryce observed the dark shadow outlined by the light of the burning ship. He got to the edge with a push of his legs and his head surfaced.

As his face broke the surface, a strand of seaweed fell into his mouth.

The salty sandy leaves and bulbous plant choked him initially, but he was able to quickly pull the seaweed from his teeth and cling to the floating S-P-Y name as if it were a raft.

Bryce's hands grasped the rough splintered, singed wooden edge and pulled himself up on it. Moving to the center of the raft, he was able to bend his knees and float, pulling the rope up behind him.

He reached out to find another smaller plank of wood and used that as a paddle to navigate toward other survivors splashing and struggling to keep their heads above water.

Although the winds had calmed, and the sea had become tranquil, the aftermath of the storm still presented a challenge to any who still lived.

Turning back toward the wine merchant's boat, Bryce saw one of the men had now lit a lantern. Perfect. He could use that point of light as a target when he was done saving these poor souls.

That small point of light was a welcomed diamond brilliant in the black velvety night. A beacon of hope, which would lead him to safety.

Bryce sat on this flat wooden transportation, which supported his weight well above the surface and paddled toward the sound of a struggling survivor.

Once there, he would hand them a portion of the rope and tell them to pull themselves to the nearest bag, filled with cork and cling to it until one of the rowboats arrived to collect them.

Bryce would then whistle as loudly as he could to get the attention of one of the rowboats. Once they shouted in reply they were heading over, he would paddle to the next person.

Over and over, Bryce Aiden Tyler wove a ropy web of cork-filled bags amongst smoldering ember-edged bits of debris, which had fallen from the Spy to the water below.

Bit by bit, Bryce found a victim, whistled, then instructed them to cling to the cork-filled sac, reminding them help was on its way.

As soon as one of the rowboats yelled that they were heading toward Bryce's whistled signal, Bryce would paddle away searching for the next victim in need.

The rowboats would reach the survivors, pull them aboard, and once the tiny vessel was full, would then row back to the docks. Once on shore, each group of survivors could be greeted with warm dry Dutch-made blankets, and Susanna Wright. Then, the rowboat would return to find more souls.

One by one, each victim of Henry Mossop's enslaving schemes were saved. This took Bryce a goodly amount of time.

One crewman had now spotted the paddling Bryce Aiden Tyler on top of the wood which contained the name of the destroyed ship, The Spy. This volunteer shouted a report to the others. Bryce Aiden Tyler was alive.

This news of Bryce's progress seemed to unify the volunteers in their efforts with renewed vigor. They adjusted sails, and the rudder, checked that the anchor still held, and even made the lantern brighter for Bryce to see.

"I think he's found another one!" One of the men shouted as he kept the sail in position.

"Good thing," another added, "As he's been out there for a couple of hours. He must be exhausted."

"And there goes another, jumping overboard!" shouted the other, working to keep the wine merchant' boat steady.

A volunteer said, "The rowboats are finding them. Do you hear that? Mr. Tyler is whistling when he finds a soul. He's alerting the rowboats... That's how they are filling up so quickly. We have room, we can take some aboard this vessel. We are actually saving lives!"

"But," a third ventured to his comrades, "How many people can Bryce save before his energies are spent or we are overloaded and are too heavy to return to shore? How long can he continue?"

The first man barked to his comrades, "Not much of a choice: Die in flames on the ship or in the water below the ship."

Another responded, "I think that Mr. Tyler is giving them a third option: life."

Bryce had now encircled the watery inferno and sinking vessel, the Spy, one full rotation.

Now, however, as Bryce tried to move forward to make sure he was able to identify all the survivors, he found his tiny raft was stuck. He thought perhaps it was another clump of seaweed and tried to push it away with his hand.

When he plunged his arm into the depths to feel for what was blocking him,

Bryce was surprised to find pockets of air bubbling around him. Over those bubbles appeared to be some sort of fabric. It was quite heavy, this fabric. Thick and sturdy.

Could it be a porthole cover from the ship above him? Yet, this was not a luxury ship and having fabric over a porthole seemed to be an unnecessary indulgence for a ship which may have transported slaves.

He grabbed it and pulled. It was fabric. A rather large portion of it. He used his other hand to pull the next section. It was not sailcloth.

It was too fine a material. In the light of early day, just before the sun had graced the horizon, Bryce Aiden Tyler noticed a brocade weave in the fabric. Definitely not sailcloth! Instinctively he continued to tug at the fabric. It was getting heavier as if it were weighted at the other end.

Boldly, he chose to release the lead rope, which had all the cork-filled bags tied to it and he used all his might to pull this water-laden brocade fabric. While his hands were in the water, he felt silky strands drift around his wrists.

It was hair. Women's hair.

Tangled, matted with debris and seaweed, but it was the long strands belonging to the gentler sex... and she may still be alive.

Focusing on this discovery and ignoring all else around him, he concentrated on the fact that he had just found another human... a person who required him to nobly rescue despite his own peril...

He kept pulling on the fine strands with such determination that Bryce Aiden Tyler, temporary captain of the commandeered wine merchant's vessel, did not look up above him to witness the Spy ship looming ever closer... and a mass of falling debris about to crash on top of him.

7 CHAPTER 135: (JULY 4, 1776 – 7:00AM) The Boat Returns

On the docks, with survivors laying on the ground around them, Magistrate Karl Pinkney and Eliza Lucas raced. They hurried to meet the wine merchant's boat, which Magistrate Pinkney himself then dispatched again, to search for Bryce Aiden Tyler.

Now, they saw the wine merchant's boat approaching. Eliza and the magistrate looked at each other with anticipation. One of his men disembarked and hopped out to secure the boat.

He strode to Magistrate Karl Pinkney and stood stiffly at attention.

"The news, Soldier," Magistrate Pinkney demanded anxiously, "Full report!"

Behind the soldier, Eliza Lucas noticed weary survivors were being helped off slowly.

"Mr. Tyler, Sir. He devised a scheme to keep a rope afloat, but when lowered into the water, it tangled around our rudder, threatening to capsize the wine merchant's boat. Mr. Tyler jumped in and straightened it out. "

"So, where is Bryce?" The Magistrate Pinkney pressed.

"Sir, he managed to climb on some drift wood which fell from the sinking ship. He used that as a raft to get several souls to hang onto the rope and we were able to pull several aboard and others were able to hang on as we towed them back to shore here..."

45

"And where..." The Magistrate Pinkney slowly spoke, "Is Mr. Bryce Aiden Tyler?"

As the survivors were unloaded, the men lined up shoulder to shoulder with this first red-coated soldier. Eliza turned to Magistrate Pinkney after the boat had emptied, "Your Mr. Tyler and my Jane are not among these survivors, Karl."

The men looked at each other, and then looked at the ground. Survivors collapsed from exhaustion as soon as their feet touched solid ground. They still required assistance walking as most were wobbling as if they were still at sea.

Eliza pleaded with Magistrate Pinkney, "Please do not tell me that the friend of Jane Hargreaves, Bryce Aiden Tyler, who saved all these lives with his bold rash foolish decision, has lost his own life along with Jane's?" Eliza shook her head in disbelief, "No. It cannot be."

Magistrate Pinkney choked. His mouth suddenly dry.

He took a deep breath and firmly ordered, "Fully unload this boat and go back out to sea," then his voice softened, "and bring back the body of Bryce Aiden Tyler if you can find it..."

His head hung low as he sighed slowly contemplating the sacrifices everyone had made -even Mr, Tyler - to help those whom he may never ever know, yet were worthy of sacrifice because they all were in these colonies to grasp the elusive whisper... the hope... of freedom.

And freedom cost dearly.

8 CHAPTER 136: (JULY 4, 1776) Following Susanna to Philadelphia, Pennsylvania

"We have arrived!" Susanna Wright said with excitement as she looked out the carriage window.

"Is this what the Congressional Congress looks like?" Polly asked, "That building?"

Mrs. Dunlap replied, "Congress is not a building, but the collection of fifty six men who will one by one sign that document you translated, Polly. They will meet in the State House in this lovely city of Philadelphia."

Polly clarified, "In this colony of Pennsylvania."

Susanna added, "I believe other documents proposed to His Majesty in the past failed because only a few colonial representatives signed it. This is different in that we have been meeting secretly to convince all representatives to commit to the ideas by boldly drawing their signatures in ink."

Billy Dawes, sandwiched between TallMan and Silversmith. guided the carriage horses, slowing them to a walk.

Billy saw an area where several carriages had parked and he headed in that direction and found a suitable spot to halt all six of his horses. Then, the three atop the carriage climbed down and helped those inside the carriage to emerge.

"So," Silversmith spoke as she stood looking at the building mere yards away, "The center of town is where those men who had met in that barn will sign a document today, eh?"

Silversmith reached inside the carriage to hold Polly's baby while TallMan and Billy Dawns assisted the women as they descended from the carriage.

"It's the Congressional Congress building," Billy Dawes added.

"Polly, I think it best you remain here with the baby," Mrs. Dunlap spoke softly. "It will be very crowded in there and I fear for your newborn's health. I don't know how long these signatures will take."

Polly nodded. "Yes, perhaps you are correct," she reached into her bag and handed the scrolls to Mrs. Dunlap, "Here are the words penned by Robert Livingston in both English and this one in German, Mrs. Dunlap. The quill and inkwell. "

Mrs. Dunlap took them and said, "I can't wait until Berlin finds out about this. Oh, King Fredrick the Great will simply have a fit knowing his people are coming here to escape his rule."

Susanna Wright asked, "Two years ago, in 1774, didn't our King George the Third, threaten us with 'the dye is now cast! The Colonies must either submit or triumph?'"

Mrs. Dunlap continued, "Oh that was addressed to Lord North in a private letter, was it not? Yes. Well, I suppose we simply must choose the 'triumph' option."

Eunice added, "I'm quite glad to be living outside of the influence of kings."

TallMan warned, "Just because our people do not have a European king does not mean we will be immune to their corruptions and wars, mother. That is why we are here."

Eunice replied, "You are right, my son."

Mrs. Dunlap added, "Yes, I'm quite sure King Fredrick of Germany will happily accuse British King George of being a poor leader, whose affairs are always in disarray for letting us, his pets, roam wild. Oh, and that *Count Ewald Friedrich von Hertzberg* will tell the world how our colonies will never last as a united force... I just know it! Boys will fight." Mrs. Dunlap shook her head.

Eunice asked, "Have there not been other letters written to the King of the Great Empire asking him to leave your colonies be?"

Mrs. Dunlap whispered her reply to Eunice, "This document does not simply ask the King to leave the colonies alone... it demands he acknowledge that our thirteen colonies are absolutely no longer part of the British Empire."

"And that means," Susanna added, "Refusing to allow the crown to profit from the kidnapping of our colonists by enslaving them. Refusing the crown to profit from lands confiscated without just reason. Refusing to accept the crown's inferior goods into our land..."

"Last year," Polly commented as she got out of the carriage and reached to Silversmith for her bundled infant, "my husband told me that he heard Abigail Adams wrote in a letter that the dye is cast. To her she felt the sword was now our only, yet dreadful, alternative... I believe if they sign, war is inevitable... the thought of loss of life makes me fear for my son's future."

Susanna comforted, "But think how much more we would lose by doing nothing, Polly."

Polly stared at her hands, inhaling slowly as she contemplated Susanna's words.

Susanna tried to encourage Polly, "We have all lost... friends... or husbands... by permitting these power maniacs to run wild with no consequences to their selfish actions. It would be as if you permitted a two-year-old child to race about with a lighted torch, yet be surprised when your home burns down. We must convince those men to sign."

TallMan added, "Future loss of life is inevitable if we are to support freedom for generations to come. Learning to live peacefully and respecting this earth we live in, will force many to first spill blood, just as an undisciplined child will have a tantrum when told to behave."

With lively optimism, Mrs. Dunlap smiled at Polly, "Polly dear, this German translation will force King Fredrick to realize that all Europeans, all people, wish to be governed fairly and with consistent justice. The people demand that their leaders guard and protect their citizens. No longer will residents of these colonies permit their leaders to act like self-indulgent capricious irresponsible children."

"Are you using children as examples simply because I am a new mother? Well, what will happen with my German translation?" Polly asked.

Mrs. Dunlap replied, "I'm sure Robert Livingston has a document in there already, but Miss Susanna Wright here asked me to bring a copy, just in case. After the English version is signed, my husband, Mr. Dunlap and a colleague of his, tell me they plan to create a new newspaper called, the *'Allgemeine Literatur-Zeitung'*."

"Why is that?" Eunice asked.

Mrs. Dunlap explained, "After they are fully organized," Mrs. Dunlap looked up to the heavens and waved her hands, "probably in another decade or so... my husband hopes it will print stories which inform the German people." Mrs. Dunlap smiled as she continued, "Mr. Heinrich Miller, who lives in the Pennsylvania colony and prints more of a pamphlet than a newspaper, will print Polly's translation after everybody has signed it.

Have you heard of the *'Pennsylvanischer Staatsbote'*?"

TallMan, concerned about the passing time, suggested, "Should we go in?"

"Indeed," Mrs. Dunlap agreed, waving the rolled up scroll as if it were a conductor's baton as she turned to lead the others in a march toward the building where the Congress was meeting.

Polly saw the group begin to march forward and said, "The babe and I shall remain here. Perhaps we will take a stroll. After such a frightful storm, the weather now seems placid and agreeable, but..." Then Polly looked at Silversmith, "Could Silversmith and Mr. Dawes remain with me?"

"I should watch the horses and remain outside," Billy offered. "I would be most delighted to keep company with two enchanting ladies." Billy removed his cap, gave a short bow, and replaced his cap.

"I would be happy to help Miss Polly with the babe," smiled Silversmith. "We can explore that church over yonder…"

Billy added, "With the crowds entering that congress building, I suspect the church will be quite empty and I would estimate it would be but a ten minute walk from here…"

"Perfect, then," Polly smiled, "If the babe wakes and cries, it won't bother anybody trying to pray."

Mrs. Dunlap reiterated, "Then, if you are not at the carriage, we shall walk ten minutes to the church and meet you over there."

So, it was settled.

Soon, the pressing crowds swallowed up the silhouettes of TallMan, Eunice, Susanna Wright and Mrs. Dunlap. The throngs of people pushed against the four newcomers as they tried to enter the building.

Mrs. Dunlap, the most vocally observant, announced that this person and that individual were clearly disregarding public manners. A disgrace, Mrs. Dunlap pronounced on several occasions. The four were forced up a steep staircase onto an overcrowded balcony.

Mrs. Dunlap, self-appointed mother hen, looked over her shoulder to ensure her other three chicks, Eunice, TallMan, and Susanna Wright, were still all together.

The indoor balcony looked down on the meeting floor of important men below.

Mrs. Dunlap maneuvered to be at the front of the balcony, pushing others aside and pulling her three less aggressive companions along.

Mrs. Dunlap used her whalebone pannier bird cage on either hip to push her way clear in order to secure seats on the bench in the front row. She ignored the comments of those around her muttering words like "rude" and "ramp". After all, Mrs. Dunlap had just uttered similar comments about other strangers, so she was expecting to receive the same. Only when TallMan and Eunice approached, did Mrs. Dunlap flip up each side of her skirts to allow Eunice and TallMan to sit on one side of her and Susanna Wright on the other side.

It took a surprisingly long amount of time for the crowds in general to situate themselves. A few moments after Mrs. Dunlap claimed a good portion of the front bench in the upper balcony, others who had just arrived, were now forced to stand. Mrs. Dunlap folded her arms, triumphant that she had captured the last seats.

Mrs. Dunlap looked down at the men below her and leaned over to Susanna saying, "I wish Jane could have joined us. We'll have to tell her about it when we return to the Inn."

Susanna looked up at the ceiling and prayed a silent prayer about when she should tell all these people that Jane had been lost at sea in an effort to save Button.

"And what if," TallMan whispered, "if your monarch does not wish to honor your request to separate from his kingdom?"

Susanna added, "In June, just a month ago, Richard Henry Lee already resolved that our colonies, if united, would have the right to be free and independent and absolved from all allegiance to the British Crown. The colonies do not want any political connection with Great Britain."

Mrs. Dunlap leaned over and whispered, "If King George won't agree to free us from his remote governance, signing that document informs his Majesty that we will go to war. Formally."

"Indeed?"

Mrs. Dunlap nodded, with a knowing twinkle in her eye, "We want to ensure we all become free and establish our own better form of governing ourselves to protect our citizens. We will not stand for abuse from any monarchy."

A gavel wrapped louder than the buzz of conversation in the room.

Those in the balcony first heard the heavy metal bolt slide shut on the outside doors.

Then the doors leading to the upper balcony closed with a bang. All people would remain where they were for the duration of this meeting.

None permitted to enter, nor leave... Not until all matters were settled.

The meeting formally began.

9 CHAPTER 137: (JULY 4, 1776) The Balcony

The gavel had finished wrapping. The doors had been locked. The Continental Congress was now in session.

In the balcony, TallMan and his mother Eunice stretched their necks so they could observe the man at the front of the room on the lower floor.

Mrs. Dunlap, who had read the letters sent by Robert Livingston and given them to Polly Mulhoolin to translate, was fully aware and intent on listening to every syllable about to be spoken. Susanna Wright bit her lip. She had participated in all the secret meetings, which were fundamental to the development of this document.

Mrs. Dunlap whispered to Susanna, "I do hope Polly and Silversmith are managing with the baby outside."

Susanna Wright replied, "They have Billy Dawes to watch over them. He said he had to mind the horses and carriage, anyway. I think three adults can manage to care for one baby. They'll be fine. Now, shhhhhh."

On the floor below. The man at the front of the room stood up. In a deep robust voice, he said, "Gentlemen..."

Susanna wright extracted the list from her pocket. Yes. John Hancock was on that list. He needed to sign this document.

Would he? She put her list back in her pocket.

Then, she recalled, with all her commotion getting here, where was Button? He was supposed to be at this meeting!

Frantically, she looked around. The crowds were too thick to pick out faces. She shook her head.

Now, she had the burden of informing her companions about Jane Hargreaves disappearing at sea and now she was negligent in executing her original purpose of getting Button to this meeting.

She looked up and asked God to take pity on her.

The rustling and conversation halted.

John Hancock waited until all was silent before he commenced, "Our first order of business is to finalize and review the document we have been discussing at our clandestine meetings."

There was a commotion in the crowd. One attendee shouted, "We should have known about these meetings. Should have been included..."

Another man stood impatiently and replied, "We ensured every person's interests were represented, sir." And then he sat down.

"The scribe is not yet present," another stated.

Susanna Wright leaned forward, now, looking around at reactions in the crowd. She exchanged glances with Mrs. Dunlap.

"Where is the scribe? He was to bring us the document to read and sign!" John Hancock demanded. Again, there was a commotion.

Another person in the crowd shouted, "The King's men are everywhere and they probably collared him and destroyed the document before he could get here."

Noisy conversation enveloped the crowd like a blanket of frustrated confusion. Nobody knew what to do and some started to blame others for not having taken precautions to protect the messenger.

Mr. Hancock shook his head, then grabbed the gavel and gave it one loud blow on the table, causing the echoes of wood slamming against wood to reverberate against the stone walls.

He challenged the crowd with, "Are we so unorganized that we have lost the very document which threatens we will be an organized force against the throne?"

Mrs. Dunlap stood up in the balcony and against all tradition boldly spoke, "I have a copy of the document, sir, herewith."

The men below were aghast that a woman spoke and the murmur of the crowd rose to a protesting roar.

John Hancock took a gavel and rapped it until the crowd started to quiet.

"Madame," John Hancock shouted over the still boiling cauldron of angry protests slowly simmering down, "I will see this specimen. Forthwith."

Mrs. Dunlap nodded.

When she turned toward the balcony exit, she realized it was bolted and locked. She could not descend from the upper balcony to the lower floor. Even if the doors were unlocked, so many people were crowded between her and the exit that her way was blocked.

The crowd below grew impatient. Some started to throw insults.

TallMan instinctively wondered, if they protested a woman in their midst who was trying to help, how much more would the crowd protest a native of these lands dressed in the comfortable animal-skin garb of his tribe?

He didn't know how to make himself smaller, but knew an angry crowd would lash out at anything... including him.

10 CHAPTER 138: (JULY 4, 1776) Mrs. Dunlap and the Scroll

Ignoring the hum of a frustrated crowd, Mrs. Dunlap took it upon herself to consult quickly with her friends to derive a solution.

Mrs. Dunlap leaned over to TallMan and Eunice, whispering. Both looked at Mrs. Dunlap and nodded.

Mrs. Dunlap took a leather strip from one of Eunice's braids and tied it around the rolled up paper, then attached the pen that TallMan had fashioned earlier on their journey.

Mrs. Dunlap then stood up and leaned as far over the balcony as she could.

Susanna Wright gasped and grabbed her skirts in case Mrs. Dunlap leaned over too far.

Mrs. Dunlap closed one eye, aiming for John Hancock, and then pushed the scroll and feather forward. It sailed through the air, from the balcony, across the room, over the heads of the protesters and to land perfectly on the desk in front of John Hancock.

Triumphant, Mrs. Dunlap sat on the bench once more.

Susanna Wright leaned over to Mrs. Dunlap, and quietly whispered, "Good that you brought a reserve copy in English as well as the German translation."

Mrs. Dunlap whispered, "The English version is the copy Polly wrote on a piece of vellum, which her husband gave to her before he.... I didn't think we'd use it... so she could show it to her son... I mean, I thought we'd sign the German version... not the English as the English was supposed to have already been in this room before the meeting started..." Mrs. Dunlap stopped her whispering to observe the happenings of the men below on the main floor.

Eunice, now tying both her braids together with the one remaining leather cord in her hair, mouthed to Mrs. Dunlap, "Well done."

TallMan conveyed his admiration for Mrs. Dunlap's gumption with a look.

With a smile, Thomas Jefferson now slowly stood up next to John Hancock to grasp the eagle feather and the scroll, which now lay before them.

He unfurled the vellum and then looked up to Mrs. Dunlap in the balcony and announced loudly, "True Colonial ingenuity solves problems with clever solutions. I thank you, Madame." He nodded to Mrs. Dunlap in the balcony.

Mrs. Dunlap's face beamed with pride. Oh, she couldn't wait to tell her husband, John, that Thomas Jefferson thought she was inventive!

Thomas Jefferson then looked down at the attached quill, which had served as the vehicle of flight for the scroll, and recognized the pen as an eagle feather.

He held the eagle feather high over his head and proclaimed, "Gentlemen, may this feather of the eagle represent the heights to which we will soar!" Thomas Jefferson, then lowered the feather and raised the scroll declaring, "May we take this parchment... this vellum... to summarize all the tenacity and sincerity which we, the people, united, represent. We will persevere, use ingenuity, and overcome obstacles... as a united nation governed by God's hand of providence."

The crowd buzzed with excitement as they discussed the scroll, which had sailed over their heads. Words such as "united" and "providence" frequently could be discerned over the cacophony of conversations.

John Hancock continued over the hum of the crowd, "And, to set an example, I shall be the first to sign this document!" John Hancock dramatically dipped the eagle's feather quill into the inkwell near him, only to find that it was dry.

He scratched the nib of the quill on a piece of blotting paper nearby and it left no marks. The inkwell was dry.

Thomas Jefferson exhaled with exasperation, "Has anybody ink?" he asked.

Susanna stood, emboldened by Mrs. Dunlap's recent example, "I sir, have a sealed bottle here. The wax is not yet broken." She held the bottle high above her head, so it could be seen from the balcony.

"Madame? " John Hancock announced, "I fear if your aim proves to be true, that the ink bottle, which you plan to hurl may injure someone should it find its mark. However, I must commend you for being prepared when our own representatives were not." He gave a cold stare to those around him, who had been tasked to be prepared. He continued, "Should this document mark the first page of our new history as a united force, I think it best that we never ever mention these incidents."

Susanna pushed toward the balcony railing and looked over. She spotted a bearded man looking up at her in the crowd with two palms outstretched toward her ready to catch the small glass bottle.

"You may toss it here," called the man as he rose to his feet. "I am a doctor from our nearby village, so should you injure me as you toss the ink, I will be able to tend to my own wounds." He smiled, encouraging Susanna Wright to drop the ink-bottle. The village doctor scooted out of his seat, walking to the center aisle to avoid any potential of hitting somebody seated next to him. He raised his hands out to catch the ink-bottle as it would descend from the balcony above him.

As this was occurring, Thomas Jefferson turned to John Hancock and looked at the document.

Jefferson then stated deliberately to the audience, "I believe we need to make some adjustments to the words. We need to be firm about condemning the British for making slavery so easy and profitable. No monarchy has any right to promote the slave trade! It must be stopped."

Gingerly, Susanna Wright released her grasp on the bottle as it sailed down into the waiting hands of the village doctor.

The doctor caught the falling bottle of ink as Susanna dropped it from the balcony. He immediately turned to face the front of the room, striding toward Thomas Jefferson.

As the good doctor, ink bottle in hand, approached the front of the room, he suggested, "We have waited a very long time for this, Sir. Could you not have the representatives of the colonies sign it before us as witnesses. Later, if discussions of key points arise, perhaps the document can be modified and reprinted at a later date?"

Benjamin Franklin now stood up and proclaimed, "We have already deliberated for three days. Any more changes or additions must be completed, reprinted and resigned within the next fortnight." Then, he sat down, again.

Mrs. Dunlap shouted, "My husband is a printer! He can create a fresh copy by this afternoon, I am sure of it! We can have a messenger bring you a broadside today for you to authenticate, Mr. Hancock. And more copies can be made! As you wish it! When you wish it!"

TallMan cocked his head to one side, eyes narrowed analyzing, contemplating.

Then, TallMan leaned over to his mother, "That village doctor..."

"Yes?" Eunice replied, "What of it?"

TallMan inhaled slowly as he pondered a bit, "Did you see the man seated next to him? Next to the doctor? He seems familiar..."

Eunice replied, "All I see are tops of heads and hats, mostly."

TallMan muttered to himself, "The man seated next to the doctor is familiar to me. He looked up briefly, but only for a second. I cannot recall why he is familiar, since I did not see his face entirely..." He pushed closer to the balcony railing, peering over, contemplating his memories as he stared at the tops of the heads below him.

The seal to the ink bottle was broken, and TallMan's feather quill was dipped into the ink with the grand flourish, for which John Hancock was known.

John Hancock stated, "As President of Congress, I have signed. The British Ministry can now read that name without spectacles; let them double their reward. Now we must all hang together."

"Tempting fate? They are paying out five hundred pounds for your head, Mr. Hancock," Benjamin Franklin remarked as he stood up to sign the document for Pennsylvania, "But, we must indeed all hang together, or most assuredly we shall all hang separately..."

Benjamin Franklin and other representatives of the colony of Pennsylvania signed .

"Who will sign next?" John Hancock challenged after he demonstrated with an exaggerated flourish how to let the king know boldly who was supporting this document, this concept of freedom from British rule.

Hancock declared, "Do we have a representative of Georgia present? Mr. George Walton? Mr. Lyman Hall? Mr. Button Gwinette?"

11 CHAPTER 139: (JULY 4, 1776)
Waiting Outside

Outside the building where the others had entered and were now locked in, Polly enjoyed the warmth of the sun. She gently gazed at the sweet baby boy, now sleeping in her arms. Billy Dawes had dismounted from his carriage perch, and now looked into the slumbering face of this tiny angelic bundle.

"He looks like an angel, Miss Polly," Billy Dawes said to Polly. "I'm sure he will grow to be a fine man." Polly looked up and down the deserted streets around them.

"Imagine," she said to Silversmith and Billy Dawes, "every last soul in this town is inside that building… the only people I see are footmen and others assigned to tend to the carriages and horses out here."

"Oh, we don't just tend to horses when we wait for our passengers to return," Billy smiled.

"Really?" Silversmith questioned, "Well, as you wait out here, what do you think about, Billy?"

Billy Dawes shrugged, "I've been delivering newspaper supplies for John Dunlap for years. The roads are always a problem. I think that is why sending a letter is so egregious."

Silversmith asked, "Is there no solution?"

Billy nodded, "The solution could be to set up houses to store packages so they can be delivered more efficiently from one storage house to the next. This would be for packages as well as letters. Somebody needs to make sure the roads between those storage houses are in good repair. Then, delivery from one to another would be more regular even in bad weather. It would eliminate delays in delivering items."

"I think that is brilliant, Billy..." Silversmith sighed in admiration as she added, "Perhaps before we leave, you can find Benjamin Franklin and ask him. I think Miss Jane would endorse how you create such practical ideas to improve the future." Silversmith next turned to Polly and asked, "And how is the little fellow, there? Have you wondered what his future would be if that document is signed and accepted?"

Polly sighed as she looked down at the babe in her arms, "Born in a storm and delivered by a medicine man of the Bear clan," Polly mused. "I worked diligently

on that document and if it is signed...
My son and I will have an interesting
future... I wish his father could have..."
she stopped short, as she took a
deliberate breath.

"It's too soon to think about the boy's
future," Silversmith consoled, "But what
of a name?"

Polly replied, "When I married, I did
not take my husband's family name. So,
I think perhaps now would be fitting to
give my husband's family name to my
son."

Billy asked, "Won't it be difficult to
explain why you call yourself his mother,
Polly Mulhoolin, when you don't share
the same surname as your son?"

Polly thought a bit and did not reply.

"Perhaps," Silversmith said
thoughtfully, "Worry about names later.
When people come to these lands, some
have changed their names to adopt one,
which is easier to pronounce."

"Then," Polly said deliberately, "I will teach my son of justice, integrity and honor... these are all the qualities my husband... had..." A single tear pooled up in Polly's eye.

Billy Dawes suggested, "Perhaps we can all go for a bit of a walk. The fresh air on a peaceful day such as this would do us all some good."

Brightly, Silversmith suggested, "Let us venture to that church."

She looked at Billy and asked, "Mr. Dawes, you estimate it to be a ten minute walk?"

When Billy nodded, Silversmith turned to Polly and said, "It is possible seeing a saint's name could inspire you to select a name for your son...."

Silversmith looked at the baby, smiled at him, and then returned her gaze to Polly as she continued, "Or we can earnestly pray for those in that building... and all our friends..."

"And you can get a blessing for your son," Billy Dawes added. "May he produce future generations of gallant noble souls who can stand for truth, justice and the British American way."

Polly suggested, "Mrs. Dunlap said the people not only want to escape from the abuses of the British monarchy, but the German and all the monarchies, as well."

The trio and day-old baby boy wandered across the cobbled street, down a ways to the small stone church.

They reached the church and opened the doors.

Suddenly, behind them, was the raging clatter of an official carriage racing down the street, which then suddenly halted as soon as it passed Silversmith, Billy Dawes, and Polly with babe in her arms.

"Is that carriage stopping on our account?" Billy Dawes asked, moving to put a protective arm around Silversmith just in case the occupants had ill intent.

"We are the only ones walking about. All the other people are minding horses and carriages," Silversmith observed, "or are in that congress meeting."

Polly asked, "But what could they possibly want with us?"

12 CHAPTER 140: (JULY 4, 1776)
Unexpected Arrival

The carriage halted in front of the startled Silversmith, Billy Dawes and Polly.

The baby uttered a soft peaceful gurgle, but continued to sleep. The clattering hoofs from the newly arrived carriage had already startled Polly and she nearly dropped her newborn babe.

Silversmith and Polly, both occupied and focused on the task of comforting the sleeping babe, hoping he would not awaken, were too distracted to even notice passengers emerging from the unexpected arrival of this carriage.

"Silversmith!" came the voice.

Silversmith looked up as she responded to her name being called. She glanced around and her eyes rested on the woman who had just stepped down from the carriage. Her skirts were shredded and her appearance disheveled.

"Miss Eliza!" Silversmith cried out. She rushed to Eliza and evaluated her appearance, "I thought Miss Susanna was a fright, but... Oh, it matters not, it is good to see you, Miss Eliza!"

Then Magistrate Karl Pinkney likewise hopped down from what was, in fact, his own official carriage.

Eliza Lucas looked at Polly and Billy Dawes, then Eliza asked Silversmith, "Where is Susanna?"

"Oh, Miss Eliza," Silversmith started, "Miss Susanna is in that building over there."

Billy helped out by clarifying, "The Continental Congress is meeting there."

Polly added, "She is with my friends, Mrs. Dunlap, TallMan and his mother, Eunice."

Silversmith shook her head, "Oh, me manners! I've forgotten them!" She turned to Eliza Lucas and said, "Miss Lucas, this is Billy Dawes, Miss Hargreaves' carriage driver. And, this is Polly Mulhoolin, Miss Hargreaves' friend." Quickly, Silversmith added, "I've a skirt for you, over there, in the carriage. Miss Susanna brought it with her. I'll fetch it straight away."

Before the others could say anything, Silversmith dashed off to the carriage, a short distance away, to fetch the skirt from Jane's wardrobe, which Silversmith had given to Susanna at the inn. Susanna had brought it with her, but now had left it in their carriage.

Polly explained, "It's a pleasure to meet you, Miss Lucas. I think..."

Eliza waved a hand at Polly, stopping her from continuing, "Oh, just Eliza. Please call me Eliza. I think we've all gone through too much to remain formal."

"Eliza, then. Please call me Polly," Polly continued, "We witnessed warders locking up the doors. I believe they are all in that building until the meeting has concluded."

By now, Silversmith had returned, panting with the skirt in hand.

Silversmith turned to Billy, "You won't believe me, but I'll tell nonetheless..."

She started, "Right now, as I was

fetching this skirt, I saw a carriage I've seen at Mrs. Dunlap's home. It could be the one she loaned to the strangers who could not stay at the inn last night. Perhaps, Billy, you could talk to the driver and see if I'm mistaken or not?"

"I can do that, Silversmith," Billy agreed. "Is Mrs. Dunlap's driver there?"

"I did not see a soul," Silversmith replied. "Perhaps it is best to wait until the meeting concludes and all the people can return to their carriages. Then, you can tell Mrs. Dunlap she is able to collect her carriage, here, and not wait until she returns to the inn..."

"Agreed," Billy concurred simply.

Then, Eliza noticed the bundle in Polly's arms. She hesitantly asked, "Is that... a... baby?"

"Yes, Eliza," Polly announced proudly, "He came to me last night."

Eliza gasped and then stepped forward

to examine the sleeping child. "He is so tiny..." she commented.

"I think they get bigger with time," Polly giggled, "A new member of my clan..."

Then Eliza rushed to the Magistrate's carriage parked beside them and flung open the door announcing, "Polly's baby arrived. Last night! During the storm!"

The others could not see nor hear whom Eliza was addressing.

Magistrate Karl Pinkney simply stood silently by, smiling.

Then, he calmly walked to the carriage door and extended an arm to assist the unseen passenger out of the vehicle.

From beneath, her matted disheveled hair and nearly fully covered in a scratchy woolen blanket, limping, the woman emerged, barely recognizable.

The next to materialize from within the carriage, was a man, also rather disheveled.

Although speechless, Silversmith was pleased she had the foresight to have just fetched the skirt from Jane's wardrobe, which she loaned to Susanna at the inn.

Silversmith originally thought it would have been donned by Eliza Lucas, but now that she observed this other woman, Silversmith knew exactly who had to wear that skirt.

14 What Just Happened?

Bryce Aiden Tyler navigated the wine merchant's vessel and then felt himself plunged into the sea despite his efforts. Soon he found the tempest actually tossed him into the path of another victim of the churning waters, which presented him with a choice:

Should Bryce save himself?

Should Bryce reach out and rescue a limp human body floating nearby in hopes there may be breath in them, yet? Should he risk his own life for the possibility of rescuing another unknown person who may already be dead?

Bryce made his decision. He chose to endanger his own life because assisting a fellow human, who was in distress and possibly still alive, was more important to this gentleman than any selfish thoughts of self-preservation.

His focus on aiding another outweighed the fact he was risking his own life, jeopardizing his own safety. The task of rescuing another demanded such focus that Bryce was unaware of the impending looming dangers nearby. Will his friends and relatives know the risks he took or would he perish, an unknown soul, in these troubled waters?

Meanwhile, TallMan has offered a symbolic eagle's feather to help sign the new Declaration of Independence.

It was explained in the story that it was vital to have an eagle feather because of what this valiant bird represented and meant to older historic civilizations and empires.

At the same time, Susanna, travelling to Philadelphia, Pennsylvania, wants to witness the signing of this astonishing document which could change the course of history... or it could fail, deflating the hopes and the efforts of all the people who participated in getting this document to be signed by those who wish to unite behind a new idea about how to manage a nation.

Unexpectedly, Silversmith realizes that something is amiss, but she must investigate further. She wonders if any of her efforts makes a difference. No matter how insignificant you feel your role is in life, know all your contributions further a goal to achieve the better or the worse in humanity... depending on the small decisions you make. What choice will Silversmith make? Will it lead to ultimate good or ultimately disastrous consequences?

Do you think the effort you put forth goes unrecognized?

Perhaps your efforts remain dormant, like a freshly planted seed, until it grows and is harvested, which means your smaller choices forge a larger path which could make a very large impact... later... when the time is right.

Isn't it worth it to do the very best you can so that perhaps one good deed could positively impact another's life?

15 Did You Know...

In the 1770's the British crown viewed exports from America to be valuable, in particular: sugar, tobacco, wheat and rice. As the Revolution was gaining momentum, communication became extremely important. At the time, the colonies produced several (about 37) newspapers. Most were issued on a weekly basis.

Because "freedom of the Press" and journalism were so valued, even the colony of Virginia (as with others) defended the Press and documented that attitude in their local Declaration of Rights. This was signed as *The Virginia Declaration of Rights, June 12, 1776.* It declared, in part, *"assembled in full and free convention; which rights do pertain to them and their posterity, as the basis and foundation of government."*

"Article XII That the freedom of the press is one of the greatest bulwarks of liberty and can never be restrained but by despotic governments."

.This Virginia declaration also addressed:

1. (Article I) All men are equally free, can own property, and be happy, safe and enjoy liberty.

   a) Section 1. That all men are by nature equally free and independent and have certain inherent rights, of which, when they enter into a state of society, they cannot, by any compact, deprive or divest their posterity; namely, the enjoyment of life and liberty, with the means of acquiring and possessing property, and pursuing and obtaining happiness and safety.

2. (Article IV) No man should take a bribe to better his personal situation. He must always act in the best interest of the people.

   a) That no man, or set of men, is entitled to exclusive or separate emoluments or privileges from the community, but in consideration of public services; which, nor being descendible, neither ought the offices of magistrate, legislator, or judge to be hereditary.

3. (Section 8) If accused of a crime, you should be told of what you are being accused. If you have a trial, it should be fast, fair, and witnesses must testify the facts. The trial needs to be efficient. You can not be denied your liberty until you are found unanimously guilty by a jury of your peers.

a)   ...That in all capital or criminal prosecutions a man has a right to demand the cause and nature of his accusation, to be confronted with the accusers and witnesses, to call for evidence in his favor, and to a speedy trial by an impartial jury of twelve men of his vicinage, without whose unanimous consent he cannot be found guilty; nor can he be compelled to give evidence against himself; that no man be deprived of his liberty except by the law of the land or the judgment of his peers.

4.(Section 12) The Freedom of the Press means reporting facts and the truth

b)   That the freedom of the press is one of the great bulwarks of liberty, and can never be restrained but by despotic governments.

5.(Section 13) The Military should only be active during war time. Anybody who owns a gun should be trained and expected to serve during war as a soldier.

c)   ......That a well-regulated militia, composed of the body of the people, trained to arms, is the proper, natural, and safe defense of a free state; that standing armies, in time of peace, should be avoided as dangerous to liberty; and that in all cases the military should be under strict subordination to, and governed by, the civil power...

Not everybody who lived in the American colonies liked the idea of cutting ties with the King of England. Some estimate that about 20% of the colonists were loyal to the British king during the Revolution.

The number of people who lived in the British colonies in North America around the year 1770 were over two million (2,165,076).

Compare that to the population of London in the year 1775, which was about 1 million.   There were a lot of "engagements" of battle during the Revolutionary war and some estimate 1,546 military engagements.

This resulted in anywhere from 4,400 to 6,800 causalities and about 8,400 wounded. Battle wounds were not the only cause of death. There was also disease during the Revolutionary War which could account for about 10,000 additional deaths.

Additionally, some estimates say that over 8,500 American souls died in British prisons. There were over 18,100 Americans captured during the war. The British casualties were about 24,000.

So the price of freedom in the United States resulted in a tremendous loss of life.

Dunlap Broadside - July 4, 1776

16 Vocabulary

In the early 1770s, before the colonies united into the United States of America, some words and terms were used, which are explained in this section.

Allgemeine Literatur-Zeitung (p55) is a newspaper which started around 1785 by Friedrich Justin Bertuch, "the father of the German periodical."

Count Ewald Friedrich von Hertzberg (P52) Born 1725- 1795 (age 69) became a lawyer in 1745 and became a director in the Prussian state archives by 1750. This started his career to influence international politics with the goal of preserving the interests of Prussia. In 1752 he married Baroness

Marie von Knyphausen. Earlier he was hailed by his king for making peace with Sweden (1757). He also negotiated peace with the Treaty of Hubertsburg (1763) and was congratulated by the king with,"I congratulate you. You have made peace as I made war, one against many." He also took part successfully as a publicist in the negotiations concerning the question of the Bavarian succession (1778) and those of the peace of Teschen (1779). Much later he penned a letter to George Washington (14 June 1793).

Daughters Of Liberty- These were the women who wove fabric to make clothing for their families so that they could boycott the purchase of British fabrics. This started around the year 1765.

Fop or **Foppish**- "Fop" is a term for a man who is so obsessed with how he looks and the clothing he is wearing and how to behave that it overshadows everything else. It is not a flattering term.

Fortnight (p75) this is a period of time of two weeks. This was a term used in the 17th century (1600's). The Old English is ***feowertyne niht***, which means "fourteen nights". Today you may hear the term "biweekly" or every two weeks....

Middling - Before the concept of "Upper class", "Middle class", and "Lower class", people recognized status by their titles. This separated government workers from royals, or even farmers. People who held a trade were called "middling people" and may have been the start of the working class - or middle class, meaning they had to learn a skill so they could hold a job to earn money to pay the bills. They did not have an allowance or "trust fund" to pay their bills.

Pennsylvanischer Staatsbote (P55)
This is German for "Pennslyvania State Messenger", a weekly newspaper written for the German speakers who moved to the Colonies. It was designed to inform them about events. Heinrich Miller, a German-born entrepreneur who had made the Colonies his new home, reported on July 5, 1776 the decision of

the Continental Congress to accept the Declaration of Independence from the King of England. A few days later, the entire declaration was translated into German and published. The English version of the Declaration of Independence was published on July 4th, 1776 for the members of Congress. The American public could read about it on July 6th.

Scribe (p65) This was a job function. A person who acted as a scribe copied manuscripts by handwriting them word-for-word. This was before mechanical or electronic devices were invented to make copies. These scribes would also work as the secretary of noble officials, doing such tasks as dictation, bookkeeping, penning and interpreting legal documents, etc. Later this job function transitioned into public professions such as journalist, reporter, etc... This term has been used since the 12th century (1100s).

.

ABOUT Wynter Sommers

Wynter Sommers is the pseudonym for an American writing team, which harnesses multiple skills in technology, research, history and education. Formally trained with a PhD in Education, Wynter Sommers blends academic classroom experience, with corporate sophistication, and a passion for developing more effective student insights through engaging storytelling.

Wynter Sommers has a heart to inspire creativity and develop critical thinking skills, all to encourage readers to make wise choices in life.

Wynter Sommers takes each story and weaves the plot with classic gripping elements, which endure throughout repeated readings, revealing new meanings each time the story is explored. The small choices a reader makes in real life could have a lasting effect in future generations. This set of stories shows the origin of not just Bjorn Esterday and Sarah Paradise, but of their ancestors and the sort of world which was established, which unfolded in each generation until Bjorn and Sarah met.

It is rewarding to learn of heartfelt, thought provoking conversations taking place globally about the characters of these books. Should the reader be presented with extraordinary circumstances, it is the sincerest wish that they act with honor, truth and integrity to overcome obstacles in real life whilst the reader hones skills of self-reliance and collaborative teamwork despite barriers outside of the reader's control. Wynter Sommers hopes you enjoy the other *Bjorn Esterday Was not Born Yesterday* stories in this series.

www.ingramcontent.com/pod-product-compliance
Lightning Source LLC
Chambersburg PA
CBHW030036030726
47500CB00001B/142